SMART LIKE ME
I CAN BE

WRITTEN BY TIFFANY BUTLER
ILLUSTRATED BY ZEYNEP ZAHIDE ÇAKMAK

ISBN: 979-8-9862507-1-7 Paperback
ISBN: 979-8-9862507-2-4 Hardback

Library of Congress Control Number: 2022909542

This Book Belongs to:

_____

SMART LIKE ME I CAN BE
WHATEVER I WANT TO BE

A Singer

I use my voice to sing melodies and songs
to entertain people.

A Writer

I use words to teach and educate.
I write books, poetry, and stories.

An Actor on TV

I perform in movies, plays, and TV.
I dress up in fancy clothes and costumes.

A Dentist

I clean and check your teeth to make sure they are strong. I remind you to brush your teeth and floss.

A Teacher

I work in schools and colleges to help students learn new skills.

A Race Car Driver

I entertain crowds by driving cars at top speeds
to win races against other drivers.

I CAN BE WHATEVER I DESIRE

SMART LIKE ME
YOU WILL SEE
I CAN BE
WHATEVER I WANT TO BE!

A Meteorologist

I predict the weather outside like tornados, snow, rain and sunny days.

An Architect

I draw and design pictures of houses
and other buildings.

A Chef

I cook delicious food for restaurants and parties.

I STUDY AND LEARN TO BE THE BEST I CAN BE

DON'T YOU WANT TO BE SMART LIKE ME

A Photographer

I take pictures using special cameras to record special moments and events.

A Fashion Designer

I make stylish clothes using fabrics and colors.

An Air Traffic Controller

I tell pilots how to safely fly airplanes in the sky.
I tell the pilots what direction to travel and when
to safely land the plane at the airport.

An Interior Designer

I use furniture and decoration
to make houses beautiful.

SO MANY BIG DREAMS I
CAN SEE

MY FUTURE IS SO BRGHT THAT I AM FILLED WITH DELIGHT!

An Environmental Scientist

I work in a laboratory and outside to study the air, water, and soil. I make sure the air is healthy to breathe and the water is safe to drink.

An Optometrist

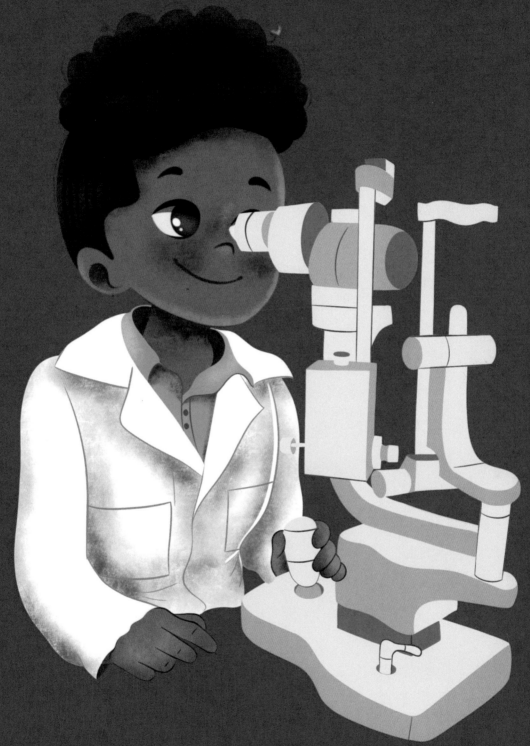

I check your eyes by performing tests to see if you can see clearly or if you need to wear glasses.

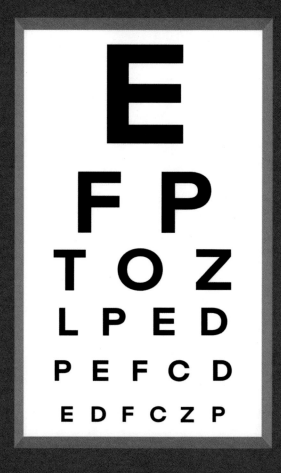

SMART LIKE ME,
YOU WILL SEE
I WILL BE
THE BEST ME THAT I CAN BE

NOW THAT YOU SEE,
ALL THAT I CAN BE LET'S THINK
ABOUT WHAT YOU WANT TO BE!

Smart Like Me I Can Be:

_____

_____

_____

_____

_____

_____

_____

_____

_____

_____

_____

_____